Lost on the Train

T0337101

Written by Catherine Baker

Illustrated by Victor Tavares

Collins

Who and what is in this story?

Listen and say

Grandma

Dad

Jasmin

Download the audio at www.collins.co.uk/839711

ticket inspector

train

platform

🎧 ② Jasmin woke up. It was Saturday morning. She was happy.

"Oh yes!" she thought. "Today I can see Grandma!"

Jasmin got dressed and cleaned her teeth.
Then she went down the stairs.
Dad was in the kitchen.

"Quick, Dad!" said Jasmin. "Let's go on the train to Grandma's house!"

"Have some breakfast, Jasmin." Dad laughed. "Then we can go on the train!"

Platform 7

After breakfast, they walked to the train station.

"Our train is at platform seven," said Dad.

Jasmin jumped on to the train! "Be quick, Dad," she said.

They sat next to a window. The train moved away from the platform. Jasmin looked out of the window. She liked all the houses, gardens, trees and birds.

Jasmin looked down. There was a teddy bear on the chair. "Look, Dad," she said. "It's a lost bear."

"Oh dear!" said Dad.

A woman came with drinks, sandwiches and cakes.

Jasmin showed the woman the bear. "It's a lost bear," she said.

"Oh no," said the woman. "There was a boy here before you. I think it's his bear."

She said, "Give me the lost bear. I can find the boy."

"Thank you," said Jasmin. "Can we have lunch, Dad?"

"No!" laughed Dad. "It isn't lunch time, but we can have a drink."

Then Jasmin needed the toilet.

"There it is," said Dad. "Be quick!"

Jasmin came out of the toilet.
She stopped. Where was Dad?

"Oh no!" Jasmin thought. "Now *I'm* lost!"

Jasmin was afraid. Then she saw a ticket inspector.

"Can you help me, please?" she said. "I don't know what to do. I'm lost!"

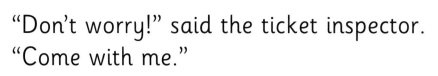

"Don't worry!" said the ticket inspector. "Come with me."

Jasmin and the ticket inspector walked down the train. Then Jasmin saw Dad.

"Jasmin!" Dad said. He hugged her. "What's the matter?"

"The man helped me," said Jasmin. "I was lost."

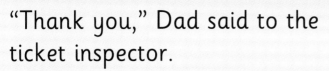

"Thank you," Dad said to the ticket inspector.

"Jasmin was a very good girl," said the ticket inspector.

19

Jasmin sat down again.

"You are clever," said Dad. "A ticket inspector can always help."

Then they saw the station for Grandma's house.

"There's Grandma," said Jasmin. "Can we have lunch now, please?"

Picture dictionary

Listen and repeat

lost

platform

station

ticket inspector

toilet

1 Look and order the story

2 Listen and say

Collins

Published by Collins
An imprint of HarperCollins*Publishers*
Westerhill Road
Bishopbriggs
Glasgow
G64 2QT

HarperCollins*Publishers*
1st Floor, Watermarque Building
Ringsend Road
Dublin 4
Ireland

William Collins' dream of knowledge for all began with the publication of his first book in 1819.

A self-educated mill worker, he not only enriched millions of lives, but also founded a flourishing publishing house. Today, staying true to this spirit, Collins books are packed with inspiration, innovation and practical expertise. They place you at the centre of a world of possibility and give you exactly what you need to explore it.

© HarperCollins*Publishers* Limited 2020

10 9 8 7 6 5 4 3 2

ISBN 978-0-00-839711-1

Collins® and COBUILD® are registered trademarks of HarperCollins*Publishers* Limited

www.collins.co.uk/elt

British Library Cataloguing in Publication Data

A catalogue record for this publication is available from the British Library.

Author: Catherine Baker
Illustrator: Victor Tavares (Beehive)
Series editor: Rebecca Adlard
Commissioning editor: Zoë Clarke
Publishing manager: Lisa Todd
Product managers: Jennifer Hall and Caroline Green
In-house editor: Alma Puts Keren
Project manager: Emily Hooton
Editor: Matthew Hancock
Proofreaders: Natalie Murray and Michael Lamb
Cover designer: Kevin Robbins
Typesetter: 2Hoots Publishing Services Ltd
Audio produced by id audio, London
Reading guide author: Emma Wilkinson
Production controller: Rachel Weaver
Printed and bound by: GPS Group, Slovenia

Download the audio for this book and a reading guide for parents and teachers at www.collins.co.uk/839711